This book belongs to:

_____

Brüder Grimm

RAPUNZEL

Illustrated by
Karin Blume

F. Coppenrath Verlag, Münster

Once upon a time there was a husband and wife who had long wished for a child. At last the woman had reason to hope that her wish would be granted.

The couple had a little window in the back of their house from which they could look down into a splendid garden filled with the most beautiful flowers and herbs. But the garden was surrounded by a high wall, and nobody dared go in, for it belonged to a powerful and wicked witch who was feared by all the world.

One day the woman was standing by the window looking down into the garden, when she saw a bed planted with the most beautiful rampion, of the kind they call Rapunzel.
It looked so fresh and green that she longed to taste it.

Each day her longing increased, and because she knew she could never have any, she began to pine and look pale and miserable.

Her husband became frightened and asked: "What is wrong, my dear wife?"

"Ah," said she, "if I do not get some rampion from the garden below, I shall die." The man, who loved her dearly, said to himself: "Sooner than let my wife die, I shall get her some of that rampion, whatever the cost may be."

At twilight he climbed over the wall into the witch's garden, hastily cut a handful of rampion, and brought it back to his wife. She made herself a salad with it at once and ate it ravenously.

The salad tasted so good, so very good that the next day her longing was even greater. If she was to have any peace, her husband must climb into the garden once more. And so at twilight he went back again. But when he got over the wall he was terribly frightened, for there, standing right in front of him, was the witch. "How dare you climb into my garden and steal my rampion like a thief?" she said with angry eyes. "You will suffer for this!"

"Have mercy on me," pleaded the man. "Only great need made me do this. My wife saw your rampion from our window and had such a strong desire for it that she had to have some, or die."

At this the witch's anger lessened and she said: "If you are telling the truth, you may pick as much as you wish, on one condition: You must give me the child that your wife will soon bring into the world. It will have a good home, and I shall care for it like a mother."

In his terror the man agreed to everything, and as soon as the child was born the witch appeared. She named the child Rapunzel and took it away with her. Rapunzel grew into the most beautiful child under the sun. When she was twelve years old, the witch locked her up in a tower that stood in the middle of a forest. The tower had neither stairs nor door, only a little window way up at the top. When the witch wanted to get inside, she stood underneath and called:

"Rapunzel, Rapunzel,
Let down your hair."

Rapunzel had magnificent long hair, as fine as spun gold. Whenever she heard the witch's voice, she loosened her long braids, wound them around a window hook, and let the hair fall twenty feet down to the ground. Thus the witch climbed up.

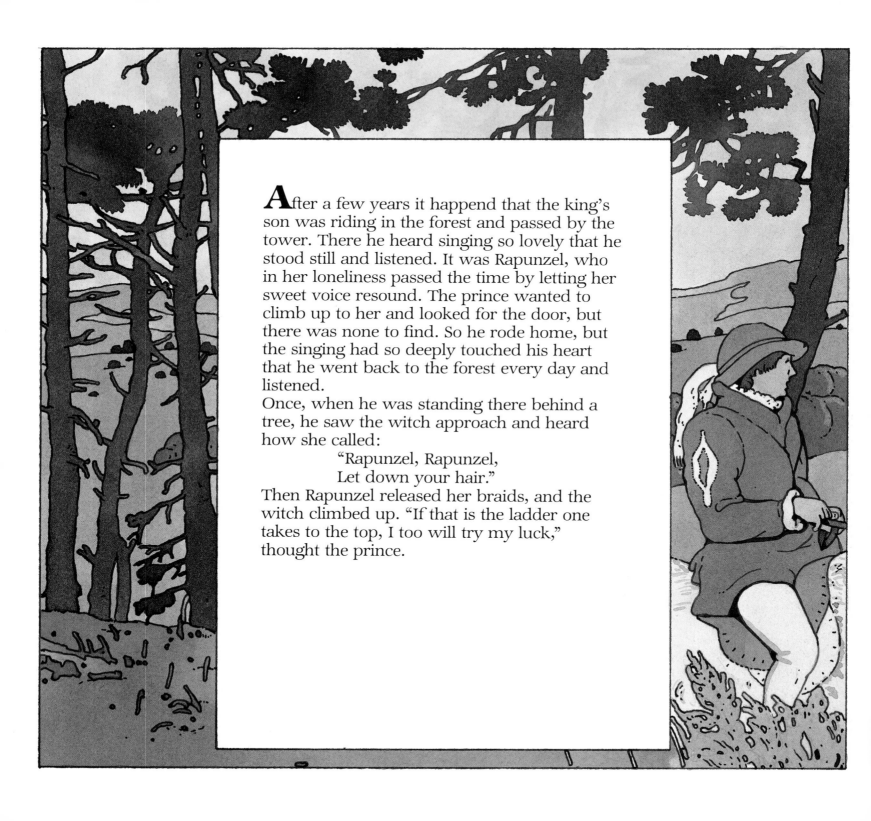

After a few years it happend that the king's son was riding in the forest and passed by the tower. There he heard singing so lovely that he stood still and listened. It was Rapunzel, who in her loneliness passed the time by letting her sweet voice resound. The prince wanted to climb up to her and looked for the door, but there was none to find. So he rode home, but the singing had so deeply touched his heart that he went back to the forest every day and listened.

Once, when he was standing there behind a tree, he saw the witch approach and heard how she called:

"Rapunzel, Rapunzel,
Let down your hair."

Then Rapunzel released her braids, and the witch climbed up. "If that is the ladder one takes to the top, I too will try my luck," thought the prince.

The following day when dark was falling, he went to the tower and called:

>"Rapunzel, Rapunzel,
>Let down your hair."

The hair came down, and the prince climbed up. At first Rapunzel was very frightened when he entered her room, because she had never seen a man before. But the prince talked to her very kindly, and told her how his heart had been so moved by her singing that he could find no peace until he saw her.

Then Rapunzel lost her fear, and when he asked her if she would like to marry him and she saw how young and handsome he was, she thought: "He will love me better than my old godmother," and said yes, and put her hand in his. Then she said: "I would love to come with you, but I do not know how to climb down from here. Each time you come, bring a rope of silk, and I will weave a ladder. When the ladder is long enough, I will climb down and you will take me away on your horse."

They agreed that until then he should come every evening, for the old woman always came by day.

The witch noticed nothing until one day Rapunzel forgot herself and said: "Tell me, Godmother, why is it that you are so much harder to pull up than the young prince? He is always with me in an instant."
"Oh, you wicked child!" screamed the witch, "I thought I had kept you from the world, and still you have deceived me!" In her fury she grasped Rapunzel's beautiful hair, wound it several time around her left hand, seized a pair of scissors with her right hand, and – – ritsch, ratsch – – the lovely braids fell to the floor. And heartless was she that she took poor Rapunzel into a wilderness and left her there to live alone in misery and want.

At dusk on the same day that she had banished Rapunzel, the witch fastened the severed braids to the window hook, and when the prince came and called:

"Rapunzel, Rapunzel,
Let down your hair,"

she let the hair down. The prince climbed up and found not his dearest Rapunzel but the old witch, staring at him with angry and venomous eyes.

"I see," she cried scornfully, "you come to catch your sweet lady, but the beautiful bird has flown the nest and will sing no more: the cat got her and soon it will scratch out your eyes too! Rapunzel is lost to you, you will never see her again."

The prince was beside himself with grief, and in his despair he leapt from the tower. His life was spared, but the thorns into which he fell pierced his eyes. He stumbled blindly through the forest, with only roots and berries to eat, and did nothing but lament and weep over the loss of his beloved wife.
He wandered in misery for years until he finally arrived at the wilderness where Rapunzel lived in poverty with the twins she had borne, a boy and a girl.

He heard a voice which sounded so sweetly familiar to him, and he went toward it. As he came closer Rapunzel recognized him; she threw her arms around his neck and wept. Two of her tears fell onto his dead eyes, and they grew clear again, and he could see as well as before.

He led Rapunzel to his kingdom where he was received with great joy, and there they lived happily with their beautiful children for a long, long time.

ISBN: 3-88547-274-0

© 1986 F. Coppenrath Verlag, Muenster
Edited by Eugenia E. Leftwich
Printed in W.-Germany
by Kleins Druck- und
Verlagsanstalt, Lengerich
Bound by Klemme, Bielefeld

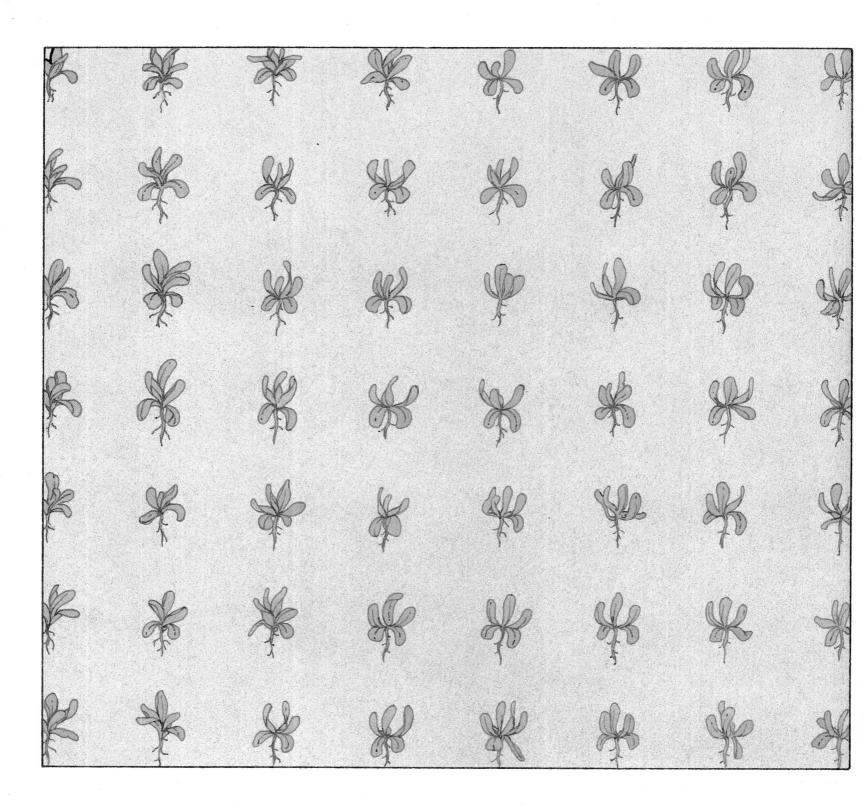